"I REMAIN IN DARKNESS"

ALSO BY ANNIE ERNAUX

A GIRL'S STORY

THE YEARS

THE POSSESSION

HAPPENING

SHAME

EXTERIORS

A FROZEN WOMAN

A MAN'S PLACE

SIMPLE PASSION

A WOMAN'S STORY

CLEANED OUT

"I REMAIN IN DARKNESS"

ANNIE ERNAUX

Translated from the French by

TANYA LESLIE

SEVEN STORIES PRESS
New York / Oakland / London

A Seven Stories Press First Edition

Seven Stories Press
140 Watts Street
New York, NY 10013
www.sevenstories.com

Library of Congress Cataloging-in-Publication Data
Ernaux, Annie, 1940–
    [Je ne suis pas sortie de ma nuit. English]
    "I remain in darkness" / Annie Ernaux; [translated by Tanya Leslie].
— 1st ed.
    p.   cm.
    ISBN 1-58322-014-3 (cloth)
    1. Ernaux, Annie, 1940- —Diaries. 2. Authors, French—20th century—Diaries. 3. Alzheimer's disease. I. Leslie, Tanya. II. Title.
PQ2665.R67Z46713   1999
848'.91403—dc21   99-41332
[B]   CIP

9 8 7 6 5 4

Printed in the U.S.A.

MY MOTHER began losing her memory and acting strangely two years after a serious road accident from which she had fully recovered—she was knocked down by a car that had run a red light. For several months, she was able to continue living on her own in the old people's residence of Yvetot, Normandy, where she was renting a small apartment. In summer 1983, in the grueling heat, she fainted and was taken to the hospital. It was discovered that she hadn't eaten or drunk anything for several days. Her refrigerator was empty except for a packet of cube sugar. Clearly, she could no longer be left on her own.

I decided to let her come and stay with me in Cergy; I was convinced that the familiar surroundings and the company of my two teenage sons Éric and David, whom she had helped me to bring up, would cause her symptoms to disappear and that she would soon become the energetic, independent woman she had been for most of her life.

This was not the case. Her lapses of memory got worse and the doctor mentioned the possibility of Alzheimer's disease. She could no longer recognize the places or people she knew, like my children, my ex-husband, myself. She became a confused woman, and would nervously roam the house, or would spend hours slumped on the stairs in the corridor. In February 1984, seeing her state of prostration and her refusal to eat anything, the doctor had her taken to Pontoise Hospital. She remained there for two months, then spent some time in a private nursing home before being sent back to Pontoise and placed in the long-term geriatric ward, where she died of heart failure in April 1986, aged seventy-nine.

While she was still living with me, I began jotting down on small undated scraps of paper the things she said or did that filled me with terror. I could not bear to see my own mother slip into such a state of decline. One day I dreamt that I screamed out at her in anger: "Stop being crazy!" Subsequently, when I got back from the hospital, I would feel this strong urge to write about her, the things she said, and her body, which I was feeling closer to every day. I would write hastily, in the turmoil of my emotions, without thinking or trying to marshal my thoughts.

Wherever I went, I was haunted by the sight of my mother in that place.

Toward the end of 1985, I began writing the story of her life, with guilty feelings. I felt that I was projecting myself into a time when she would no longer be. Also, I was torn between my writing, which portrayed her as a young woman moving toward the world, and the reality of hospital visits, which reminded me of her inexorable decline.

When my mother died, I tore up this first draft and started work on another book, *A Womans Story*, which came out in 1988. While I was writing the book, I could not bring myself to read through the notes I had taken during my mother's illness. Somehow I felt I hadn't the right: I had committed to paper her last months and days, including the day preceding her death, without realizing it. This disregard for consequences—which may characterize all forms of writing, it certainly applies to mine—was horrifying. In a strange way, the diary of those hospital visits was leading me to my mother's death.

For a long time, I believed that I would never have this text published. Maybe because I wanted to offer only one image, one side of the truth portraying my mother and my relationship with her, a truth which I sought to convey in

A Woman's Story. However I have come round to thinking that the consistency and coherence achieved in any written work—even when its innermost contradictions are laid bare—must be questioned whenever possible. Publishing these pages gave me that opportunity.

I have delivered these pages in their original form, echoing the bewilderment and distress that I experienced at the time. I have chosen not to alter the way I transcribed those moments when I was close to her, removed from time (except maybe from my early childhood regained), removed from any thought except: "she's my mother." She had ceased to be the woman who had always ruled my life and yet, despite her misshapen features, because of her voice, her mannerisms and her laugh, she remained my mother, more so than ever.

On no account should these pages be read as the objective chronicle of a patient's stay in the long-term geriatric ward and certainly not as an accusation (on the whole, the nurses were extremely caring), but merely as vestiges of pain.

"I remain in darkness" was the last sentence my mother wrote. I often dream of her, picturing her the way she was before her illness. She is alive and yet she *has been* dead. When I wake up, for a few moments, I am certain that she is still living out there under this dual identity, at once dead and alive, reminding me of those characters in Greek mythology whose souls have been ferried twice across the River Styx.

March 1996

1 9 8 3

D E C E M B E R

She just sits there on a chair in the living room. Staring straight ahead, her features frozen, sagging. Her mouth not quite open but gaping slightly, from a distance.

She says, "I can't put my hands on it" (her toiletry bag, her cardigan, whatever). Things seem to slip away from her.

She has to watch television now. She can't wait until I have cleared the table. At this moment all she understands is her longing.

Every evening David and I take her upstairs to bed. At the point where the floorboards become carpeted, she lifts her leg up high, as though she were wading into water. We laugh, she laughs too. Later on, after she had snuggled down into bed, gay as a lark, and knocked over all the things on her bedside table by trying to apply some face cream, she says to me: "Now I'll go to sleep; thank you MADAME."

The doctor came round to see her. She wasn't able to say how old she was. She clearly recalled having had two children. "Two girls," she added. She had slipped on two bras, one on top of the other. I remembered the day when she found out that I had been wearing one without her knowing. The shouts. I was fourteen, it was one morning in June. I was wearing a slip, washing my face.

My stomach pains have started again. I no longer feel anger at her and her loss of memory. A wave of indifference.

We went to the shopping mall. She wanted to get the most expensive handbag in La Bagagerie—black, made of leather. She kept saying: "I want the best one, it's my last handbag."

After that I drove her to the department store La Samaritaine. This time, it was a dress and a cardigan. She walks slowly, I need to help her along. She chuckles to herself. The salesgirls give us strange looks, they seem embarrassed. Not me; I stare at them defiantly.

She asked Philippe anxiously: "Who are you to my daughter?" He snorts: "I'm her husband!" She laughs.

J A N U A R Y

Invariably, she mistakes my study for her bedroom. She opens the study door just a crack, realizes it's the wrong room and gently closes the door; I see the latch spring up, as if there were no one on the other side. Mounting panic. In one hour, the same thing will happen again. She has no idea where she is.

She hides her soiled underwear beneath her pillow. Last night, I thought of the blood-soaked panties she would stuff at the bottom of the dirty laundry pile in the attic, leaving them there until washing day. I must have been seven years old; I would stare at them, fascinated. Now they are filled with shit.

Tonight, I was marking essays. Her voice rang out from the adjoining living room, loud and clear, like an actor on stage.

She was speaking to an imaginary child: "It's getting late, sweetie, you'd better run off home." She was in a merry frame of mind, giggling away to herself. I put my hands over my ears, I felt that I was losing touch with humanity. We are not on stage; THIS IS MY MOTHER TALKING TO HERSELF.

I came across a letter she had begun writing: "Dear Paulette, I remain in darkness." She can't write any more now. The words seem to belong to another woman. That was one month ago.

FEBRUARY

At mealtimes, her conversation suggests she is employed on a farm where my sons are hired workers and I'm the manager. She won't eat anything except cream cheese and sweet foods.

My niece Isabelle came to have lunch last Sunday; she burst into laughter every time my mother made some incongruous remark. Only we have the right to laugh at my mother's insanity, we being myself and the boys, not her. Not outside people. Éric and David say: "Granny's really too much!," as if she were still extraordinary in her condition.

14

This morning she got up and, in a timid voice: "I wet the bed, I couldn't help it." The same words I would use when I was a child.

Saturday, threw up her coffee. She was lying in bed, motionless. Her eyes were sunken, and red around the edges. I undressed her to change her clothes. Her body is white and flaccid. I started to sob. Because of time passing, because of the past. And because the body which I see is also mine.

I don't want her to die. I'd rather she were crazy.

Monday 25

We waited in the emergency room for two hours, with my mother lying on a stretcher. She wet herself. A young man had tried to commit suicide by taking pills. We went into the examination room and they laid my mother down on a table. The intern rolled up her chemise to reveal her stomach—the thighs, the white vagina, a few stretchmarks. Suddenly, I felt I was the one who was being exposed in public.

I thought back to the cat who had died when I was fifteen; she had urinated on my pillow before dying. And the blood and bodily fluids I had lost just before my abortion, twenty years ago.

M A R C H

Thursday 15

In the corridor of the hospital—or rather, I should say the nursing home attached to the hospital, second floor—I suddenly hear: "Annie!" She's calling my name, she has been moved to a different room. How could she have made out my figure from a distance, she can barely see (because of her cataract). As I walk into the room, she says, "I'm saved." She probably means, "now that you're here." She tells me a whole bunch of stories, giving me all the details: the work she is forced to do without being paid, without being given anything to drink. A lurid imagination. At least now she always recognizes me, which wasn't the case when she was staying at home.

Saturday 17

Greets me frostily. Scowls: "I don't enjoy your visits! How can you behave like that, aren't you ashamed?" I am stunned; I have just spent all night with A, making love. How COULD she know? Once again, that sinking feeling, that childhood belief that her eagle eye can see everything, like God in Cain's grave. She adds: "I don't believe it, you must have been drugged!" Later on: "Well, seems to me the world is going crazy." I laugh, slightly relieved. No woman will ever be this close to me, it's like she's inside me.

Sunday 18

Seven o' clock in the evening; she was already asleep. I woke her up. She thinks that the woman sharing her room is a little boy who has drowned in a water tank: "The *gendarmes* just sat there on a bench, they made no attempt to save him." Suddenly, she remarks: "So, the wedding's in a fortnight, right?" (Ironically, I'm seeing my lawyer tomorrow to file divorce proceedings.)

Tuesday 28

Her gnarled hands. The forefinger sticks out at the knuckle; it resembles a bird's claw. She crosses her fingers, rubs them together. I can't take my eyes off her hands. Without a word, she takes leave of me to go and have dinner. As she walks into the dining room, I am "her." Such pain to see her life end this way.

A P R I L

Wednesday 4

I have settled in her armchair, she is sitting on a chair. A chilling impression of dual personality. I am both myself and her. She has filled her pockets with bread—her longstanding obsession with food, her fear of being deprived, of going hungry (she used to store sugar lumps in her pockets and handbag). She complains that there is no one to talk to, that men are interested only in chasing women. Things that have haunted her all her life.

Sunday 8

Last Friday I was interviewed on the television show *Apostrophes*.

Today she was in a different room with two bedridden ladies, both silent. She had been tied to her armchair. Her eyes were hurting and she kept applying saliva to her eyelids. She told me that there had been a hold-up that night but "they spared our lives, that's all that matters." I untied her to walk her along the corridor and show the nurse her eyes. I so hate seeing her naked flesh when I lift her up and the hospital gown parts at the back.

In the corridor, through a half-open door, I glimpsed a woman with her legs in the air. In the next bed, another woman was moaning just like one does during orgasm. Tonight everything was surreal and the sun was beating down.

Saturday 14

She is eating the strawberry tart I have brought her, picking the fruit out from the custard. "They have no regard for me here, they make me work like a slave, we're not even fed properly." Her perennial obsessions, her fear of poverty which I have long forgotten.

Opposite us, an emaciated woman, a phantom from Buchenwald, is sitting on her bed, her back straight, a fearful expression in her eyes. She lifts up her chemise and you can see the diaper sheathing her vagina. Such scenes inspire horror on television. Here it's different. There is no horror. These are women.

Easter Sunday

When I get there, she is lying in bed. I shave her face. The two other women remain silent. The place reeks of urine and shit. It's very warm. I can hear shouts from the adjoining room: it's Madame Plassier, who used to share my mother's room at the hospital. Then suddenly you realize, it's Easter! Cars are zooming along the highway. Heading back home after a sunny weekend. The woman closest to my mother is lying on her bed, with one hand resting on her belly. It's beyond sadness.

Thursday 26

Painful moments. She thinks that I have come to take her away and that she is going to leave this place. She is bitterly disappointed, she can't swallow anything. I am overcome with remorse. Yet, occasionally, I feel serene: she's my mother and somehow she's not quite my mother anymore.

Heard the stand-up comedian Zouc: "You have to wait until people die to make sure they have lost their hold over you."

Sunday 29

I shave her face and cut her fingernails. Her hands were dirty. She's perfectly lucid: "I'll stay here until I die." And then: "I did everything I could to make you happy but you weren't any happier for it."

Tuesday 8

My mother was lying on the bed, a tiny figure, her head thrown back like on the Sunday afternoons of my childhood (did I really hate that?), her legs up in the air (did I hate that too?). She was wearing a diaper. Ashamed: "I put it on to avoid making a mess." Angry, too, with no regard for the Christian virtues she once praised: "To have worked all one's life and end up like this!" Those mad, glassy eyes. The features are definitely hers—the nose and the lips with their pretty, even contours.

My mind went back to May 8, 1958, twenty-six years ago. I had gone into town in the pouring rain to meet Guy D. He never turned up. I was wearing a thick woolen coat and carrying a red umbrella.

When I got into the elevator to leave, she was standing in front of it. When the doors snapped shut, she was still talking. An unbearable moment.

Sunday 13

Here, in Us[1], it's worse than at Pontoise Hospital. The nurse on duty says reproachfully: "She's wet herself and messed up the whole room."

I am appalled at my own cruelty. I made my mother put on her corset and stockings. She laces up the corset clumsily. Her legs are thin; she has been dressed in a pair of Petit-Bateau interlock panties. She obeys me fearfully. The scene haunts me, I keep seeing my mother with that demented expression; I desperately feel like crying but the tears won't come (maybe only after her death?). My sadistic streak reminds me of the way I behaved toward other little girls in my childhood. Maybe because I was terrified of her.

Thursday 17

I went over to fetch her at Us. She has been allocated a bed in the long-term geriatric ward at Pontoise Hospital. This may be the last time she is driven around in a car; she doesn't realize it. When we reach the hospital car park, her face crumples. I understand then that she thought she was coming back to my place. Now her room is on the fourth floor.

---

[1]Village in the Val-d'Oise *departement* where my mother was sent to a private home.

A bunch of women circle us, addressing my mother with the familiar *tu* form: "You're going to be in our group?" They are like kids talking to the "new girl" at school. When I take leave of her, she looks at me in panic and confusion: "You're not leaving, are you?"

The situation is reversed, now she is my little girl. I CANNOT be her mother.

Friday 18

She was sleeping in her slip. The crisscross of blue veins on her chest. The skin on the inside of her arms creased like the underside of a mushroom. I wake her up gently. Later, she hurls a stream of abuse at her roommate, a fat, docile woman. The nurse comes and speaks to us; he's a young bearded man with a casual, laid-back attitude. After he has left, my mother turns to her roommate with envy: "Are you happy now? You finally got to see your little doctor friend!" Ever and always, men on her mind—and thank God for that. A virtuous woman consumed by longing.

Tuesday 22

"I dreamt of Victor Hugo; he had come over to visit the village. He stopped to speak with me." She laughs as she evokes her dream. Singled out by the great poet, chosen, how typical of her.

Her face is becoming puffy, her features are changing. I had brought her some cider at her request. They came to tell me in solemn tones that all alcoholic beverages were strictly forbidden.

Friday 25

Her second pair of glasses has gone missing. I ask her what she has done with them, she falls asleep. For the first time I touch her like a child who is sleeping. Outdoors—the month of May. The May dew, which she would collect on a flannel and rub onto my face to soften my complexion. At my First Communion, in May, she had taken the collection in a black suit, a wide-brimmed hat and high-heeled shoes with straps, "a fine figure of a woman." She was forty-five years old. I'm one year younger. She was sleeping with her eyes open, her alabaster legs uncovered, her vagina exposed. I start to cry. The old lady next to her is forever making her bed, folding then unfolding the blanket. Women.

JUNE

Sunday 3

She is in the dining room, seated opposite another woman whom she is observing with a sinister smile, a cross between curiosity and sadism (when and where have I seen her smile that way?). The woman's eyes are misty with tears, she seems mesmerized by my mother and her perverse, inquisitorial expression. Today all the women are crazy. The one now sharing my mother's room kept shouting, "Please, give me some buttered bread!" Another one was muttering to herself in the corridor. A frenzy of activity, strange and mysterious.

Thursday 7

"Having to end my days here," every time I come. Still fiercely envious of my mother-in-law: "If it had been Raymond's mother (she probably means Philippe, my husband), sure they would have found room for her at home." The old lady sharing my mother's room terrifies me. As soon as I walked in, she screamed: "I want to go to the toilet!" I took her to the bathroom. When she comes out, she starts shouting again, waving her diaper, and insists that I help her on with her panties. I do what she asks. She also needs to have her nose blown. My mother looks on and says: "She's impossible. She's had three children already."

Friday 15

When I arrived, she was sitting near the elevator, looking frantic. She spoke so quietly I could barely hear her. In the corridor leading to her room, she walked with hunched shoulders. She crumbled her cookie onto the floor. I feel like crying when I see how badly she needs my love because I cannot satisfy her demand (I loved her so desperately as a child). I think of how badly I want A to love me now, just when he is drifting away from me.

When I take the elevator to go downstairs, I catch sight of her face framed between the two doors that slam shut, seemingly blotting her out with a bang.

The same visits, over and over again: we sit facing each other, exchanging a few sentences in a semi-coherent way. I know all the other patients. One of them, a youngish woman with a proud bearing, constantly paces the corridor with quick, short steps. She reminds me of the broken clock in Ravel's opera, *The Child and the Enchantments*. Today I discovered that she has a husband—sixty-something, with reddish eyes, dressed in a navy suit.

A nurse yells into the phone: "Is anyone dying?"

In the hall downstairs, an old man in pajamas is always busy making phone calls. The other day, he showed me a piece of paper with a telephone number. I dialed it for him, it was the wrong number. He spends all day trying to get hold of someone, maybe one of his children or an organization. Hoping, every morning.

The little old lady next to my mother had snot running onto her blouse. My mother was in a state of complete apathy; she hadn't even noticed. She has cut herself off from other people. She mislays all her personal possessions but has quit looking for them. She has given up. I think of the frantic efforts she would make to find her toiletry bag at my place; she still had a hold over the real world through her belongings. I am dismayed by such indifference. Everything she once owned is gone. Her watch and her eau de cologne have vanished. Now meals are all she has left.

I always see the same few visitors.

J U L Y

Thursday 12

Back from Spain. She stands up abruptly from the table when she sees me walk in through the dining room door (years ago, at boarding school, waiting in the closed-in playground, I would jump to my feet as soon as I made out her figure reaching the top of the stairs: the same surge of excitement). She announces proudly: "This is my daughter!" The women around her murmur: "She's beautiful!" I can see how happy she is. We go downstairs into the garden, sit on a bench. I recalled that when I was ten, we had both been to visit an uncle who was recovering from a prostate operation. It was at the Hotel-Dieu Hospital in Rouen. The sun was shining, men and women were walking around in maroon bathrobes: I was so sad and so happy that my mother was with me, a strong, protective figure warding off illness and death.

We took the elevator to go back upstairs. In the mirror, I could see both of us, she with her hunched shoulders. What mattered was that she was standing beside me, alive.

Thursday 26, Boisgibault

It occurred to me that she had never pampered nor shown

any love for her own body. She had never touched her face, her hair or her arms the way I do, or slipped her hand into her blouse. A worn-out body. She would collapse onto a chair at the end of the day.

A violent woman, with only one system of values to account for the world, that of religion.

I'm not sure that I could write a book about her in the same vein as *A Man's Place*. There was no true distance between the two of us. Rather, a sense of identification.

AUGUST

Saturday 11

I feel intense satisfaction at the prospect of visiting my mother today, as if I were about to learn some fundamental truth about myself. It's crystal-clear: she is me in old age and I can see the deterioration of her body threatening to take hold of me—the wrinkles on her legs, the creases in her neck, shown off by her recent haircut. She is still prey to her fears, she has never ceased to feel alienated: "The boss isn't easy to handle, we're underpaid for all the work we do" and so on. She munches the food I have brought her.

Food, urine, shit: this combination of smells hits one as

soon as one leaves the elevator. Quite often, the women go two by two, with one assuming the dominant role. For instance, there's a tall, upright woman who makes her companion—a small, stooped figure shuffling along in her slippers—walk the whole length of the corridor, then back again in the opposite direction. The place is a cage. My mother is a solitary figure.

When I take the elevator to go downstairs, I glance at myself in the mirror once again, just to make sure.

Monday 20

Now when I come to see her, I'm still young, I have a love life. In ten or fifteen years' time, I'll still be coming to see her but I too will be old.

Today she was wondering what she might buy—clothes, trinkets, whatever. But she can have *nothing of* her own. The outfit she is wearing is the one provided by the hospital, so much easier to clean when it gets soiled. She has lost all the clothes she had brought with her, as well as her glasses, of which she took such good care at my place six months ago. Here, the things that get lost are never found. No one cares: they're going to die anyway. The head nurse—tall, haughty, with black hair in a pageboy style.

The clock-lady went up to an elderly man, took his hand, raised it to her lips, then walked on. Two old ladies holding hands were strolling along the corridor; twice they stopped to greet me: "Good day, Madame!" They seemed to have forgotten they had already done so or maybe they didn't recognize me.

Friday 24

I intend to give the clothes my mother left behind at home to Le Secours Catholique, a charitable organization, or to sell them at the flea market in Pontoise. Guilty feelings. The sewing basket where she kept her needlework and buttons, her thimble—these are the things I shall keep.

I must not give in to emotion as I write about her.

Wednesday 29

I realized that I forgot about her in between visits. She said: "I hope he'll take to the water."—"Who's that, mummy?"—"The goldfish I hope to have one day." Later on, she remarked: "I'm afraid my condition may be irreversible." Her hands and body were cold as marble. And that crazy expression.

Monday 3

I read through *Cleaned Out*, which is shortly coming out in paperback. At the end of the book—a portrait of her by me, aged five. In those days I used to call her Cubby.

Wednesday 5

Indoors, the same warm temperature, all year round. There are no more seasons. All the women in their striped or flowered aprons are metamorphosed into maids. One of them, a tall, imposing figure with a queenly bearing and a shawl, reminded me of Proust's Françoise.

My mother inquires: "Don't you get bored at home?" When she talks about me, she really means herself. God, she must be so bored! Or has the word lost all significance for her? What does she actually remember about her life? What does life mean to her now?

Tuesday 11

I dreamt of her, she had wet her panties. The first time it happened in real life, it was a tremendous shock.

Every time I visit her, her face needs shaving. At the fête of the Communist Party, I was standing next to a transsexual with bluish skin. Subconsciously, I thought of my mother.

Today she couldn't understand any of my questions. "Are you getting enough sleep?"—"Yes, yes, it's perfectly clean." Giving a detailed account of everything she has done that day: I went shopping downtown, the streets were crowded and so on, as though she were leading a normal existence. Such a vivid imagination to make up for her condition. Before I left, she snapped: "It'll be ages before I get to leave this fucking place."

Monday 17

Shaving her face, cold but alive, and seeing her blank expression, I wondered: "Where are the eyes of my childhood, those fearful eyes she had thirty years ago, the eyes that made me?"

When I entered the dining room, she was feverishly wiping the table with the palm of her hand.

In her flowered apron, she looks like Lucie, the woman who came to clean for us in Lillebonne and who had lost all her teeth. My mother too has lost all her teeth, her dentures have gone missing.

In the mail this week, there was a letter addressed to my mother. *France Million—When Luck Comes Your Way*. Beside a photograph of Anne-Marie Peysson, all smiles, you could read: "Is Madame Blanche Duchesne the lucky person to whom Anne-Marie Peysson will hand over a 250,000 franc check?" At the bottom of the page, there was a facsimile of a check made out to my mother and the words: "The exceptional digital portrait of Madame Blanche Duchesne," a portrait that "comes to life when seen from a distance of one meter." At that distance, one could make out the contours of a young face with pouting lips. My mother's name was mentioned dozens of times, to convince her that she had been chosen, that she would be the winner if she replied before October 5. Assholes. Someone should grab Anne-Marie Peysson by the scruff of her neck and drag her to the geriatric unit of Pontoise Hospital.

Sunday 23

On the train, a few days ago, a nun with shiny, bulging eyes was staring at the other passengers. The face of the Inquisition. I thought about my mother uneasily.

The nurse told me that she was always talking about me, and only about me. Guilty feelings. I have also noticed that she often thinks she is me.

I was born because my sister died, I replaced her. There-fore, I have no real self.

Saturday 29

When I walked into the dining room, they were all watching television. *Only she* looked up: she spends all day waiting for me.

Worse was to come, something I could never have im-agined. I opened the drawer of her bedside table to make sure she still had some biscuits. I saw what I believed to be a cookie and took it. It was a human turd. I slammed the draw-er shut in utter confusion. Then it occurred to me that if I left it there, someone would find it, and that subconsciously, I probably wanted this to happen so that they could see how low my mother had fallen. I found a piece of paper and went to flush it down the toilet. I recalled a scene from my childhood: I had hidden some excrements in my bedroom cupboard because I felt too lazy to go downstairs and use the outdoor toilet.

Today nothing she says makes any sense: "They've changed all the 'a' and 'o' in words" and "Marie-Louise comes to see me quite often." Marie-Louise, her sister, has been dead for twenty years.

Sunday 7

Now I come and see her on Sundays. The television is broadcasting Jacques Martin's show *L'École des Fans*². Children are singing. The old people stare blankly at them. When my mother and I entered her room, my nostrils were assailed by the overpowering stench of shit. We sat down opposite each other. As usual, the other old lady was yapping, "Please, give me some cake." No one ever comes to see her. As I walked toward her, I noticed a huge pile of shit by her armchair. The nurse on duty assures me that neither the old woman (who wears a diaper), nor my mother could have done that. Apparently, an elderly man wanders around the hospital, slips into a room and defecates onto the floor.

Once again, I try to reach the elevator and get it to start before she catches up with me, before the doors slam shut in front of her face. Such distress at seeing her in her present condition. Yet she can still arouse anger in me. At the local baker's this morning, a woman gave a little girl a resounding smack. The child, humiliated but proud, does not cry. The mother's face is harsh, with a strained expression. The scene

---

²A Sunday afternoon program in which kids are invited to the studio to imitate their favorite pop singer.

upsets me; it reminds me of my own mother, who would slap me for the slightest little thing.

Friday 12

I thought back to the time when my mother was staying with me, between the months of September and February: I was (subconsciously?) cruel toward her, panicked at the idea that she was becoming a woman without a past, a frightened woman clinging to me like a child. However, it wasn't as bad as today. At least she showed longing and aggressiveness.

For the first time, I have a clear picture of what her life must be like in this place, in between my visits: the meals in the dining room, the waiting. I am accumulating bags of guilt for the future. But letting her stay at my place would have meant the end of my life. It was either her or me. I can remember the last sentence she wrote: "I remain in darkness."

I can't face wearing the garments she left behind, her bed jacket and so on. I just want to keep them, like exhibits in a museum.

I am constantly comparing my mother to other elderly women—their complexion, the state of their legs—to see "how far gone she is."

Friday 19

Vivid memories of the corset she used to wear, which encased the lower part of her body, from below her breasts to the swelling of her buttocks. I could see her cleft through the crisscross of laces.

Thursday 25

I read *The Confessor's Handbook,* an old book given to me by A. I remembered the expression in her eyes when I was a child: she was the confessor.

Sunday 28

"Acolyte" was a term she liked to use when referring to some of our customers' drinking companions. To show people that she knew complicated words. This woman never could take humiliation.

Flashes of me, aged sixteen: boys, hoping for wild love, continually. And her, my guardian: "You're far too young! You've got plenty of time!" But one never has enough time.

Writing a book about one's mother inevitably raises the issue of writing.

Monday 29

She looks even more withered and confused. All she is
wearing is her hospital gown, open at the back, exposing
her spine, her buttocks and the mesh of her panties. A
glorious sun is beating down through the double-glazed
windows. I think about my room at the students' hostel
twenty years ago. Today I am here with her. We have so
little imagination.

The little old lady needed to go to the can, wobbling
on her crooked, spindly legs, squealing as usual. She spent
a long time in there while I sat beside my mother. I recalled
the spell of gastroenteritis I had suffered in tenth grade; I
was reading Sartre's novel *Nausea*. Like the old lady, I sat
hunched over my swollen belly. It was a cold, sunny month
of February.

Wednesday 31

She's been on my mind these last few days because it's one
year since "things started happening," in other words since
her health began to deteriorate.

I dreamt of our house in Cergy which has become public property (a common occurrence). A cleaning lady dressed
in a raincoat (my mother's double?) was walking through the

garden. She appeared before me and I told her: "Stop being crazy!"

Fleeting memories: my mother's cousin, a butcher near Rouen, who would say to her in jocular tones: "I'll whip you under your blouse!"

NOVEMBER

Sunday 4

As I walk through the door, the little old lady sharing my mother's room is standing behind her bed, relieving herself onto the floor. Then she bursts into tears: "I've wet my panties." In the dining room, one of the women is always singing, describing what she does in the third person singular: "She's putting away the laundry la la la." So much pale flesh.

Saturday 24

I feel like throttling my mother's roommate because of her continual high-pitched whining. I had bought some slippers for my mother, explaining to the salesman that I needed several pairs for her to try on. His mother too is suffering from Alzheimer's; he talks about it in a low voice, he is ashamed. Everyone is ashamed.

I shaved her face and clipped her fingernails. We tried on the slippers. She seemed terrified, afraid that I would get mad at her for not understanding my instructions, "push your toes in" and so on.

It was my mother's illness, and later my affair with A, that reconciled me to humankind, flesh and pain.

One image haunts me: a big window wide open and a woman (myself) gazing out at the countryside. A springtime, sun-drenched landscape that is childhood. She is standing before a window giving onto childhood. The scene always reminds me of a painting by Dorothea Tanning—*Birthday*. It depicts a woman with naked breasts; behind her, a series of open doors stretch into infinity.

DECEMBER

Sunday 2

My mother has a sort of dark shadow over her face. Yes, it's coming back to me now—it's the same expression I saw on the men from the old people's home where my schoolmates and I would go bawling carols a few days before Christmas. She won't sit down but collapses sobbing into my arms.

She often speaks of the dead as though they were still with us but she never says a word about my father.

Sunday 9

There are clocks all over the place, in the hall, the dining room and the bedrooms; none of them gives the right time: six o' clock instead of four o' clock... Do they do it on purpose?

My mother's color is fading. To grow old is to fade, to become transparent. Zacharie the cat, aged twelve, is colorless too. Today she imagines there are other people in the room: "Don't worry, they're only customers, they'll be gone in a few minutes; half of them don't even pay their bills." Words from the past, words from our life.

The little old lady has gone, her shelves are empty. I dare not ask what has happened to her.

Christmas Day

When I received the Prix Renaudot, a literary award, she said to the nurses (they have just told me about it): "She always had the gift of the gab." Then she added: "If her father knew, he'd tell everyone about it. He positively doted on her!"

I clipped her fingernails; she moaned, despite the fact

that I always take great care not to hurt her. I can feel the sadistic streak in me, echoing her behavior toward me a long time ago. She still loathes me.

I remember she used to say: "I never asked anyone for anything in life."

Monday 31

She remarked: "They haven't said anything about discharging me. I wonder if I shall ever leave this place. Maybe I'll stay here..." She paused and didn't say, "until I die." But that was the meaning. It breaks my heart. She is alive, she still has desires, plans for the future. All she wants is to live. I too need her to be alive.

At one point: "Claude never goes to see his mother. She doesn't live far, though, she's only at Sainte-Marie." After a short pause, she reflects: "She must be out of her mind." The equation fills me with guilt: Claude = me. Claude, Marie-Louise's only son—both alcoholic, both dead.

This morning I read an article on motherhood and infertility in the newspaper *Le Monde*. The maternal instinct is tantamount to a death wish.

J A N U A R Y

Sunday 6

On New Year's Day my mother and the other patients had been dressed in their former clothes, a skirt and blouse. They were given a glass of champagne. A parody of real life. Just imagine that morning. The nurses whipping out slips and dresses from drawers and clothing the weary bodies, shouting, "Happy New Year! Let's celebrate! Come on, Granny!" All day long, they pretended to be having fun. The women seem to be vaguely waiting. There is nothing to wait for. Come evening, off go the skirt and blouse. Like when you're a child, and you dress up in costume to go to a make-believe party. Here, it's all in the past; there are no more real parties to look forward to.

   She used to say: "You must fight to survive." And

also: "If you're not strong, then you've got to be smart."
Everything in life was seen as a struggle. I speak of her in
the past tense. Yet the woman who stands before me today
is the same one I knew in the past. That's what is so terrible.

Saturday 19

All her energy is channeled into eating. Passionately,
voraciously.

In early January, I had that dream in which I am lying in
a stream, caught between two currents, with long tapering
plants floating beneath me. My loins are white; I have the
impression that they are also my mother's, it's the same body.
Shall I ever dare to analyze that?

"Who's that singing?" one of the women asks time and
again. Yet she probably hears her every day; only one of
them sings, always the same one, singing away her life.

FEBRUARY

Friday 1

As I enter the department store Les Galeries Lafayette, I catch
sight of a woman talking to herself, maybe asking me for

something. I hurry past but glance at her, she glances back. Blue-gray eyes. Afterward, I think, that's my mother, that's the way she used to look at me before. Stirrings of guilt.

Saturday 2

It's one year day for day since I met A and I find my mother tied to her armchair. "I thought you'd never come." I untie her, we walk up and down the corridor, I tie her up again before leaving (we have no alternative, the nurses insist). Just like I used to strap my kids into the stroller.

One of her favorite sentences: "After all, you only live once" (to eat, to laugh, to buy things). And, to me: "You expect too much from life!"

Saturday 16

She was at the far end of the corridor, feeling the rail running along the wall, unaware of my presence. Later, in the bedroom, she searches through her neighbor's belongings (yet another woman, the fourth since she was moved here). The bathroom floor is sticky with dried urine. Urine is everywhere, impossible to get rid of that sweet, cloying smell. Before leaving, I take her back to the dining room (I was about to write "refectory," like at boarding-school). A nurse with a cheery smile hands her a sweet: "Go on, have one, it'll give you something to do." Sheer compassion.

Museum of Fine Arts, Lille, a few days ago. A contemplative atmosphere, empty rooms guarded by an attendant. We tend to think of attendants as crazy people (they spend all day cooped up there on their own, with no one to talk to). Saw *Time and the Old Women* by Goya. But that's definitely not my mother. Neither is the main character in Lolleh Bellon's play *Tender Relations*, which I went to see the other night.

My mother went through menopause the same year in which her own mother, my grandmother, died, one month or two weeks before that "fearful Sunday," the Sunday when it happened—June 15, 1952. Around June 25, she gets back from the doctor's. My father alluded to a possible pregnancy: "So, maybe it's not the last time we're celebrating Communion?" But she knew. No, I've gotten the dates mixed up, it was in late May, after the renewal of the vows, that she went to see the doctor. So, she had stopped menstruating for at least two months. She was forty-five years old. What happened that Sunday occurred *afterward* and may be ascribed to the fact that she had stopped having her period. I can still see my father's smile and contentment at the thought that my mother might be expecting. A huge disappointment, to be sure. In those days, people would talk about a "change of life;" they would say, "I'm through with that" or "that's all over now." It seemed that everything had come to an end.

After my grandmother's death in July 1952, she invariably dressed in black or gray. It was only eighteen years later, in Annecy, that she took to wearing colors again, red suits and so on.

Saturday 23

She has lost the lower half of her dentures. The nurse on duty remarks: "It doesn't matter, she only eats blended stuff!"

Today she was in high spirits. (It's worse.) We walked up and down the two corridors. In one of the rooms, an old lady was holding up her skirts; you could see the garter and stockings. Later on, when I walked past the same room, she was standing in profile. Her buttocks were all shriveled. Another old lady called me over and asked me to pick up her mentholated drops, which she had scattered all over the floor.

M A R C H

Saturday 2

The elevator door slides open: she is standing right in front, next to an old lady. They are all the same, forever seeking out each other's company.

In such circumstances, how could she possibly find her dentures.

Every time I leave the hospital, I need to listen to music at full blast as I drive along the highway. Today, amid exhilaration and despair, I chose Léo Ferré's hit *C'est Extra*. I need to feel sexy because of my mother's body and her life in the hospital.

She would often say, "Caught you!" doing this or that. Watching me all the time.

Sunday 24, Paris Book Fair

I went to see her before going up to Paris. I feel absolutely nothing when I am with her. As soon as the elevator door snaps shut, I want to cry. Her skin is getting more and more cracked, it badly needs cream. Now she has lost the upper half of her dentures. Without her teeth, she looks like the elderly nurse from the old people's home in Yvetot, old father Roy, in his blue coat. So weak she can hardly walk. Yet she still shows an interest in my clothes; she always feels the fabric, "it's lovely." Pointing to my black swallowtail coat: "When you're through with it, have a thought for me!" Words she used to say, words from the past.

Sunday 31

She loves and hates the same way as before, fiercely, has made "friends" and "enemies." All the patients here recreate a "civilized" world: a woman is seated at the entrance, greeting people who go by with a chirpy "Good Day!" as though she were sitting on her doorstep in the street. Another old lady says to my mother: "You're far prettier than me, you've got youth on your side!"

A P R I L

Monday 15

Her face has changed. The space between her mouth and her chin is growing longer, her lips are becoming obscenely thin. All she thinks about is leaving this place.

In the dining room, the television is on, continuously (is it less tedious for the staff?). One woman had removed the waxcloth and was folding it up like a linen tablecloth. Another patient was being lowered down in the hoist.

Friday 19

I can't bring myself to give away her clothes or sell them off at the flea market. Today I sold a set of Restoration armchairs and a sideboard table which my husband and I had acquired after taking out a loan. Parting with these objects means nothing to me. Like my mother, I am letting go of things. The people who bought this antique furniture are young "executives," like we were at the time.

Sunday 21

Confined to her wheelchair once more. She vainly tries to eat her dessert, an apricot mousse: her hand can't find her mouth, her tongue keeps darting toward the inaccessible treat. I fed it to her, like I used to feed my own children. I think she realized this. Her fingers are stiff (are they overprescribing Haldol?). She began tearing up the cake box, trying to eat the cardboard. She tore up everything—her napkin, a slip— struggling to *twist* things, oblivious of her own strength. I look at her sagging chin, her gaping mouth. I have never felt so guilty; I felt that I was the one to have induced her present condition.

Saturday 27

She is looking much better although she can walk only short distances. She doesn't need any help with her cake. Afterward, she wants to wash her hands. I take her to the bathroom. "I might as well use the toilet too." She has difficulty removing the stretch panties, encumbered by diapers: "They put on too many of them." I help her to take off her panties and to put them back on. A child. Period. She says, "You'll have to bring some old rags for me to wipe my bottom with." Adds: "I went to see Dad's grave but I never made it, they were driving in the wrong direction" (naturally, she wants to live, she doesn't want to be reunited with him). "There wasn't a speck of dust on his tombstone, it's a marble slab."

Shouts from the adjoining rooms. An old man keeps repeating, "hello, hello." It might well be the same guy who was always trying to call people from the phone in the hall downstairs. A woman gives a curious squawk, mimicking an exotic bird, *tacatacata*. Today it was like a concert, life fighting to go on, breathing more fiercely than usual.

I remember the first days of my affair with A last year, when my mother's health began to slip. Back then, her face was not puffy like it is today. One evening, I watched her fall asleep: it was early evening, the sun was still out. I cried but somehow I felt I wasn't unhappy.

MAY

Saturday 4

She hadn't been able to walk for days. I had a hard time lifting her out of the wheelchair. After that, she had no problems making her way along the corridor. Guilty feelings: she starts walking again as soon as I'm with her. I gave her some doughnuts and a bar of chocolate; she stills snaps the pieces into two (so that they last longer, she would say). At one point: "How long will I be staying here? I'll be dead before then!"

Her neighbor, who is suffering from the same condition, but in the early stages, walks around with her toiletry bag all day. She lays it down on her bedside table, carefully puts it away into a drawer, then takes it out again. That's exactly what my mother used to do at my place. Having something to connect one to the real world, something of one's own.

When I was twelve, I would spend hours lovingly admiring and touching a manicure set made of black patent leather. We had so few possessions: every one of them was a dream.

She never wanted me to spend the school holidays with friends of hers. Was she afraid they might find fault with me? Or might not like me? Or—this has never occurred to me before—might she have been jealous? I would be furiously jealous when she addressed my cousin Colette or my friend Nicole as "my lollipop" or "my sweetie." Those girls weren't her daughters, she had no right to speak to them like that.

It's almost one year since she lost her glasses.

Saturday 18

Today she was in a state of total apathy, refusing to *see* me. It was a lovely day; we went downstairs into the garden, with me clumsily pushing her wheelchair. I realize that I have come to accept her degradation and her new, distorted features. I recollect that terrible moment when she began "going downhill." She kept going round in circles, searching the house for imaginary objects. (Later on, I was reminded of the tortoise we had in our garden at Annecy, who would scuttle along the gravel paths and barbed wire fence in early fall.) It was then that she wrote: "I remain in darkness."

Pentecost

As I park the car, I notice quite a few patients sitting outside in wheelchairs and some other people whom I assume are visitors. I go upstairs, my mother is standing in the corridor, she recognizes me, I wheel her downstairs into the garden. I realize that the old people are all patients from the geriatric unit, sporting ridiculous straw hats and minded by the nurses. My mother's chin seems to sag a little more every week, wrinkles have started to radiate from the corners of her mouth. We just sit there on a bench. She eats her cake. It strikes me that I never bring her the "right sort of cake"; today it's a brittle slab of shortbread oozing with jam which she gets all over her fingers. I shouldn't bring her anything except fruit jellies and almond buns. Some of the women are talking to themselves. An old man is vigorously shaking his head beneath his straw hat. My mind goes blank.

J U N E

Sunday 2

Mother's Day. I have brought along the straw hat she used to wear. We went down into the garden, sat on a bench. She didn't need a wheelchair today. Maybe, for other people, she has come to resemble a witch—her gradual metamorphosis since she came here one year ago. She is bent double, she who walked so straight. Her skin, spared wrinkles for so many years, is a crisscross of lines. Today she is holding a corner of her gown, clutching it. In the elevator, she stood facing the mirror. I am sure that she could *see* herself.

Sunday 9

She was waiting for me in her wheelchair, opposite the elevator.

She talks about suicide, money and church mass, which she can no longer attend. "I'm afraid I may have to stay here for years." Sometimes I leave my sentences unfinished. "You know what I mean," she would say when she was trying to find the right turn of phrase.

The lady next to her spends half an hour tidying her shelves, taking out all her belongings and putting them back again. My mother went through the same motions when she was living with me, at the beginning of her illness. What is the meaning of such behavior? To impose on the outside world some form of "order" that cannot be achieved inside?

How many Sundays have I spent sitting opposite her, watching her eat? Trees gently sway in the window.

She would announce cheerfully, "Annie, you've got a visitor," when a schoolfriend came round to see me. "Visits" meant a lot to her. A token of love, proof that we exist for other people.

Sunday 23

She was sleeping in the raised chair used for minor care and dressings in the hallway, her mouth wide open. My mind goes blank whenever I come here.

The old lady in her room is always carrying around her handbag, as though she were walking down the street. She brought another patient back to the room; the two women sat down side by side and just stayed there, saying nothing, exchanging polite smiles. Two little girls playing at being grown-up women on a social visit. It's heartrending.

Peals of laughter could be heard coming from the kitchen. A typical summer Sunday afternoon in the long-term geriatric ward.

Memories flash through my mind. I can see her in our grocery store, telling customers that Mademoiselle B, who had given birth to a child whose father was German, had no layette ready for the baby. It was only years later that I realized the full implications of her remark which, although suggested, were never openly stated: the girl may have been planning to get rid of the child.

Other memories, sentences from the past: "I don't have four arms!" (whenever my father or I would ask her to do something). And also: "You're not strong enough to..." She was always going on about her own physical strength, an asset in our world; I was a mere "weakling." Inferior to her.

Sunday 30

In the garden, I stand up and walk away, leaving her in the hands of the nurses sitting by some old ladies and a drooling grandpa. At that point she shouts, "Annie!" She hasn't spoken my name for over a year. On hearing her voice, I freeze, emotionally drained. The call has come from the deepest recesses of my life, from early childhood. I turn around and walk up to her. She looks at me pleadingly: "Take me away!" All the other people have stopped talking and are listening. I would like to die; I explain to her that I can't do that, not right now. Afterward, it occurred to me that she may have shouted my name because of the people around her. But I'm not so sure.

When she'd had enough of her brioche, she hid it under her skirt. As a child, I would steal candy from the store and stuff it inside my panties.

JULY

Sunday 7

She stopped walking two Sundays ago. I have gotten used to the wheelchair. I take her downstairs into the garden. It's a hot day. "The sun is nice," she says. It always takes me by surprise when I hear her use the same expressions as before, in her present state. She can't see things clearly now. At one point, she grabbed my leg and my skirt, savagely. Two young nurses sit down away from the patients to have a chat. A third nurse, older and hideously ugly, stays back with the group. My mother is wearing a printed dress with small flowers, like the ones I wore when I was a little girl. It makes her look tiny. I realize that it's only now that I have truly grown up.

She said, "See you next Sunday" although I won't be coming for two months on account of my operation. An operation which might cause me to die before her.

I told the boys about her strange attitudes and expressions. We burst out laughing. Pain cannot be kept intact, it needs to be "processed," converted into humor.

Today I was feeling guilty, yet again. So I tried to alleviate her condition by clipping her nails, which were filthy, and by washing her hands and shaving her face. I wonder if she has become incontinent now that she moves around in a wheel-chair. I didn't dare ask her.

AUGUST

Saturday 17

I haven't been back to see my mother although I am perfectly able to walk with crutches. I won't go to this temple of old age hobbling "like an old lady."

My mother—her energy, her constant anxiety too. I feel the same tenseness, only in my writing.

My father used to say of her admiringly: "You'll never have the last word with her!"

Monday 26

I went over to see her with David, who is obviously very upset. The familiar smells, her bedroom with the chimney sweep from Annecy, the statuette of Sainte Thérèse—everything in its place. Such permanence almost brings me comfort. Seeing her, touching her—she is so different from what she used to be and yet she's definitely "herself." The dining room was full of old ladies, the same ones. Rock music blaring from the television set. When I come here, I feel that I should be writing about these things instead.

SEPTEMBER

Thursday 5

Tomorrow it'll be two years since I collected my mother from the old people's home in Yvetot. I remember dropping by her flat in the Béguinage area; a woman to whom she proudly announced, "I'm going to stay with my daughter!"; conversations in the car.

Today I came to see her with Éric. She was in the hall downstairs, groping her way along a pipe running across the wall. I recognized her slippers. Her roommate was strutting around in the heat in a fur coat, dangling her handbag; she looked just like an old whore.

Her fingernails are too long and so is her hair, giving her an unkempt appearance. I don't have the energy to cut either. When I reflect on her gradual decline, I no longer "feel" anything and I have almost given up wondering whether it is "because of me." She had already started losing her faculties in 1982 before she came to my place. But I failed to give her the support she needed, she remained "in darkness" alone.

In *Le Monde*, Claude Sarraute wrote, "One was worth a million." This was one of my mother's expressions, as was "one was worth a dozen." I hated these locutions, which I saw as old-fashioned. Showing consideration, choosing one's words so as not to hurt people's feelings, were alien to her.

For me, she is the personification of *time*. She is also pushing me toward death.

Saturday 7

I used to dress up wearing her clothes. "I'll tell my mother!" She was the avenger, the one who might pick a fight with the other girl's mother.

I can remember the "cup of tea" at the dentist's surgery in Rouen. We were waiting in a room with huge armchairs and glass cabinets filled with grimacing Chinese figurines. The waiting rooms of my childhood are strange, terrifying places where I am transported to the "other world," the world of rich, important people, a "window display" that I am not allowed to touch. My mother was talking in a low voice. After an unusually painful visit, the dentist announced: "I think this calls for a cup of tea!" I am amazed that such a vile beverage should be seen as a reward and naturally expect my mother to reply, "She doesn't like tea!" Instead, she says nothing and smiles. She knew that in "high society" drinking tea was "the thing to do."

Friday 13

My mother has fractured her hip bone. Panic. Last night, seagulls were continually circling above the house, then the terrible screech of a bird rang out, a barn owl or maybe a seagull. Strangely enough, I had just been thinking of writing a book about her. I am in a state of total disarray.

Evening. I saw her; she was sleeping, mouth wide open. An urinary catheter. Her hands were twitching. I cried. I feel that all this has been going on for a long time. What can she feel? She will recover, in other words, slowly waste away between her bed and her wheelchair. I saw no one—no doctor, no nurse—in the ward where she has been moved.

Sunday 15

She has been returned to her familiar surroundings. Strapped into her wheelchair: her body tense, straining to stand up, full of vigor, her eyes unseeing. She is incapable of eating on her own, the right hand groping toward the left. It suddenly occurs to me that if society follows its present course, people like my mother may not be left alive in twenty or fifty years' time. I have no views on such an eventuality, on whether or not it is justified.

"You're overdoing it," she would say disapprovingly. My face was flushed, I was breathless with so much running around and shouting. And if I stared at her: "Do you want to buy me or something?" Gathering all her favorite sayings when she can barely speak. But she still has her *voice* and, occasionally, expressions that are so typically "her" merge to form a single identity. I vainly try to pin them down. Her obsessions: work, alcohol (repressed), horrific events, disasters and so on. She had never wished to set herself boundaries but because of her working-class background she had adopted those of religion and puritanism, seen as the nearest thing to dignity. Personally, I have never cared about boundaries.

Frightening to realize that I have always seen my mother as a figure of death. When she made the pilgrimage to Lourdes on her own, I was convinced she would deliberately die there. Later on, I was terrified by the account she gave of my sister's death: I feel that I too shall have to die before she can start loving me because that day she said, referring to me, "She's not nearly as nice as the other one (my sister)."

She will never again wear the clothes left behind at my place; they seem to belong to a dead person. Yet she is alive and can still make me feel guilty.

I notice that I have inherited her brusque, violent temper, as well as a tendency to seize things and throw them down with fury. A pointed this out to me. I also detect a similarity between some aspects of his behavior and my mother's obsession with tidying when she was at my place, almost two years ago. He keeps sorting and moving around the books in his library, drawing comfort from his intellectual possessions, making up for his terrible feelings of inadequacy for not having gotten past his *baccalauréat*. My mother was trying to cling to the world, to persuade herself that she wasn't crazy. The days when she was staying with me seem far away already. Fond memories of that time: she would start sewing and lose all the needles. Now...

I was brimming with love for her when I was eighteen; she was a big, warm sanctuary. At the time I was suffering from bulimia.

Thursday 19

The other day, she warned me she was going to be sick. I began watching her, just like I used to watch Éric when he was a little boy and pretended to throw up the food he didn't want.

I have never seen a photograph of my mother as a child. The first one was taken on her wedding day. In another one, dated a few years later, she is attending a wedding. Heavy-set face, low forehead, bull-like features. One sentence sums her up: "She was the sort of woman who burned up life" (leaving behind no papers, no traces).

She preferred giving to everyone, rather than taking from them. Maybe to get attention, to be acknowledged? When I was a little girl, I too liked to give—picture cards, candy, whatever—to be loved, to be popular. Not any more. Isn't writing, and my particular style of writing, also a way of giving?

A scene from my childhood. She is standing, naked, facing my father who is lying in bed. He scoffs: "Not a pretty sight!" Her genitals—*The Origin of the World*[3].

She would scold the dirty old men in the café: "Off with you, ugly old man" (the same applied to the dogs chasing our bitch in heat).

OCTOBER

Friday 4

I may have invented or embroidered the story she would tell people about Lourdes—a liquid mountain into which

---

[3]Painting by Courbet depicting the open thighs of a recumbent woman.

one sank and drowned when one didn't know it was water. I believed she would die there.

The expression: "I am an only child."

Her taste for using convoluted words to "show off."

When I saw *The Ostrich's Eggs* by Roussin on television, I imagined all those women I hated, the exact opposite of my mother, with their delicate bodies and porcelain features, their silk and pearls, their fancy expressions.

Tuesday 8

She is standing in the hall; at first, I don't recognize her. Her hair has been pulled back into a ponytail, there is a fixed expression on her face. I show her the little chimney sweep above her bed, a present from a friend in Annecy. She gazes at it and murmurs: "I used to have one like that." I am always wondering how she sees the world now. When I think of the woman she used to be, her red dresses, her flamboyant temper, it makes me cry. But usually, I think of nothing, I am here with her, that's all that matters. At least I still have her *voice*. Voice is everything. The worst thing about death is the loss of voice.

She would say: "So-and-so, or such-and-such a dog died of ambition." To die of ambition refers to the trauma of separation, of being far away.

Tuesday 15

A gray October day like in 1962 when I took my teachers' training certificate in literature. We sit facing each other. She is eating a custard tart; her hands are shaking, she keeps shifting the cake from one hand to the other. "I was ravenous, haven't eaten for days. I was deprived." Deprived—the usual understatement, meaning short of money. Several sentences arouse feelings of guilt in me: "It would be great to spend Christmas *back there*" and "It doesn't take you long to get here," in other words, you should come more often.

When she sees me walk in, she greets me the same way she used to greet visitors: "Gee, I was wondering when you'd come!" The same enthusiasm and joie de vivre as before. An old lady inquires anxiously of her: "You're not leaving, are you?"—"No, I'm not leaving," she is quick to reply, to avoid upsetting her, if only slightly.

Friday 18

I gave a coin to the blind beggar on the market square, like she used to.

She would say, "She made that man stray from his duty" or "one must do one's duty in life." I shudder at hearing such things, and that word in particular, and have since adolescence.

My fantastic vision of her: a glimpse of her white coat, her shopkeeper's coat, hovering behind me.

Monday 21

With other people, she was always afraid to let silence set in. "Have a word or two for each customer."

I have no idea what she thought of sex or how she made love. On the face of it, sex was the ultimate evil. In real life?

Wednesday 23

Today she says to me: "I'm sure I'd be happier with you rather than outside of you."

Her polite remarks, said out of habit: "Wouldn't you like to sit down?" to one of the nurses who is standing nearby. I began reading a newspaper. Her hands reached out for the cake wrapping and I gave it to her—like to a child. One minute later, I glanced up and saw that she was eating it. She wouldn't let me pull it away from her, fiercely clenching her fist. An agonizing reversal of roles between mother and child.

NOVEMBER

Sunday 3

The disheveled hair, the hands searching for each other, the right grasping the left like an unknown object. She can't find her own mouth; every time she tries, the cake ends up to one side. The piece of pastry I put into her hands slips out. I have to pop it into her mouth. I am dismayed at such degradation and bestiality. A glazed expression, the tongue and lips protruding, sucking like those of a newborn baby. I began combing her hair and then stopped because I didn't have an elastic band to tie it back. She said: "I like it when you do my hair." Everything was forgotten. With her hair combed and her face shaved, she became a human being. It gives her such pleasure when I brush her hair and arrange her clothes. I remembered that when I walked in the woman next to my mother was stroking her neck and legs. Being alive is being caressed, being touched.

Monday 11

She is in a state of extreme agitation, she keeps trying to wrench away the bar of her wheelchair. She clutches it and pulls with all her might, her body straining with the effort.

This violence reminds me of the aggressiveness she showed toward everything around her, including me. Suddenly I hate her, once again she is the "bad mother"—brutal and inflexible. There's a suffocating smell of shit; I don't know when I'll be able to change her myself. I fed her small pieces of cake; she didn't even glance at me. Today she would never say, "this is my daughter," on seeing me walk in, like she did last year.

Memories of her squatting on the bucket we used as a chamber pot, relieving herself shamelessly: that curious intimacy between girls which she imposed on me as a child and which I came to loathe later on in life.

Forever insisting on the notion of pride: "How can you take that?," in other words, how can you accept being treated that way? (By my husband.)

Wednesday 13

Yesterday, in Yvetot, my aunt and cousins said: "You really take after your mother, don't you; you look just like your mother!" Speaking of her, my aunt remarks: "She worked hard all her life. She would scrub the floors, saying to your father, 'leave that, I'll do it.' " She always took such pride in her sheer physical strength and her contempt for ill-health, which she dismissed as a failing. A working beast. I hated it when she said, "You're such a weakling!

Sunday 17

My mother and the little old lady sharing her room were
sitting side by side. A sweet picture illustrating a secret, magic
bond between the two of them. A biblical scene basking in
an extraordinary light, reminiscent of an Italian Renaissance
painting. A moment of pure, indescribable bliss. My mother
points to me and asks her companion: "Do you recognize
her?" As usual, the other woman stammers; she hasn't said
anything intelligible for months. It doesn't really matter
whether or not they communicate by language. I sat down
opposite them and fed my mother an éclair—the other
woman didn't want any—then a second one. From time to
time, I nibbled a small piece. Sounds from the television
filtered through, Viennese waltzes. I thought about all those
Sunday afternoons spent in Yvetot. It's not just the notion
of time passing, it's something else, something linked to
death: now I belong in a chain, my life is part of a process
that will outlive me.

I wipe her mouth with a face cloth. She looks at me and
asks, "Are you happy?"

I go to the bathroom, the floor is sticky with urine. I au-
tomatically associate it with that morning's scene at A's place.

I know absolutely nothing about her sex life. She used to say: "If people knew that, we'd be mortified."

Sunday 24

The way she sometimes looks me up and down, haughtily, as though I were a perfect stranger. She manages to eat the éclair on her own, getting it all over her fingers. Yet it's probably the pastry which she finds the easiest to eat. A song from the sixties on television, "since you're getting married tomorrow," something like that. My life since those days. And my mother, who has been so much a part of my life, always.

She smells bad. I can't change her. I sprinkle her with eau de cologne.

DECEMBER

Sunday 1

She couldn't find the way to her mouth, her hand kept wandering off to the right. I helped her to eat her cake. When her fingers were empty, she continued to raise them to her lips. I wonder if a child does that; I can't remember.

When I write down all these things, I scribble away as

fast as I can (as if I felt guilty), without choosing my words. Today she was wearing an old flowered bathrobe with all the threads pulled out. For a split-second, my mother appeared to me wearing the pelt of a wild beast.

She has finished the fruit jellies. If I leave the box on her bedside table, she won't touch it or try to pick out one of the squares. Now all she wants is to grab things or tear them apart.

The woman with glasses was in tears, sobbing, "I want to die." By her side, her husband, the one with reddish eyes, replied softly: "But you're making *me* die." He may be right. In one of the rooms, a woman was squawking like a duck being chased round a farmyard.

Before leaving, I made her drink some water. She says, "You'll have your reward." The word kills me.

Driving back home along the highway, I can still smell her eau de cologne on my fingers. Suddenly, for no particular reason, memories cross my mind—the Yvetot fair and outings with her. Could it be the smell of her face powder?

Now I often catch sight of that black shadow on her face. When I was a little girl, for me she was a white shadow. How could I have forgotten that she used to call me her "white doll" up to the age of sixteen?

All that I have standing between me and death is my demented mother.

Sunday 8

She turns to face me, her mouth wide open, her hair tied back. A flowered gown. And still that smell. I can't change her and I dare not disturb the nurses and paramedics who are chatting in the office. I can hear them talking. One of them keeps saying, "that's the problem" and "going through all that for nothing" (I think she means saving money).

She has trouble finding her mouth with the first cake. The second one she can eat on her own. So there is *still* room for improvement. The long-haired male nurse with liberal views (he calls himself an "idealist") came to look at the beauty spot on her head at my request. It had been bleeding.

Sunday 15

She is in the dining room, in her wheelchair, the only woman to be turned toward the wall. The ceiling has been decked out with tinsel. She points to the decorations and says to me, "That's Annie's dress." I am always on her mind. The wallpaper here suddenly reminds me of the kind we had in the café at Yvetot before 1950. I feel that nothing has really changed since my early childhood and that life is simply a series of scenes interspersed with songs. I settle in front of the television set with the rest of them. Behind my mother, an old lady is chuckling to herself. Another one, slightly less deranged, shouts out to her: "Quit laughing! You're crazy!" Then she takes an interest in another, completely senile woman who is pestering an elderly man in a wheelchair. Continually on the alert. By the window, I make out the old guy who was always trying to call people who never answered. Then I hear a deep voice belonging to a man (which one?), a *wild* voice coming from his guts. Voices revert to their primitive state here.

A Santa Claus figure stares back from the far side of the room. Jacques Martin's show, quizzes, some guy won a trip to America. The woman on the alert shouts, "Oh! My God!" Then they showed sexy, painted toenails: a glossy commercial. I imagined a whole lifetime—childhood, adulthood, old age—lived out in front of television and its immutable images: glamour, youth, adventure.

Sunday 22

I am sitting opposite her, a box of chocolates on my lap. Her greedy instincts are back, she leers at the chocolates, tries to grab them with clumsy fingers. After eating each candy, she wipes her mouth carefully. My seat is lower than hers, I must raise my head slightly. I am ten years old, I look up at her, she's my mother. It's the same age gap, the same ritual.

As I leave: "Why don't you take me home with you, it would be more fun."

F E B R U A R Y

Sunday 2

Since I decided to tell her story, I have been unable to write anything after returning from the hospital. Maybe now I don't need to. But its mostly because I am caught up in her past, her history.

However, I am seized with panic whenever I think of her. I am afraid she is going to die. Sometimes I even think of moving her back home. The same mad impulse which led me to take her to my place in 1970, and then in 1983, only to realize that living with her was impossible.

Wednesday 12

When I entered the room, she was hunched over her

wheelchair, staring into space, with one hand stretched out in front of her. Reaching out, touching. So typical of her, that urge to carry on exploring the outside world. Today she could eat on her own, with either hand. Gets thinner and thinner every day. Each time I visit her, I notice some small detail that upsets me and highlights the agony of the situation. Today it was those long brown socks they have to wear, the ones which reach up to their knees and which are always falling down because they are too baggy.

I did a curious thing: lifted her gown to see her naked thighs. They are painfully thin.

As soon as she laughs, she's her usual self.

It was a cold, sunny day. I can't get away from that landmark, the beginning of her illness: "two years ago..." Back then, she would go out walking with our dog Maya; ask to see a lawyer; go upstairs to bed with the boys at night.

Thursday 20

I am finding it more and more difficult to cope. Because I am writing about my mother's childhood and adolescence, I can "picture" her in my mind, radiating energy, beauty and warmth. And then I go and visit her, like today, and catch her in her sleep, mouth gaping, all skin and bone. I need to shout, "Mummy, it's me!" The two images are incompatible. In my writing, I am heading toward the moment when she will be confined to her wheelchair in her present state. Suppose she were no longer there, suppose life were to outpace fiction... I don't know whether I am engaged in giving the kiss of life or the kiss of death.

Cake Day. "The Thursday ladies are here!" chants one of the nurses. Cakes are handed round by volunteer workers— two for each patient. Now I remain calm when she spits out the pieces of custard tart that are too big for her. I cut them up into smaller pieces. Her skinny body scares me. Maybe they have lost patience trying to feed her. She says: "With you, I'm in safe hands."

M A R C H

Sunday 2

I have the impression that she has been the same for some time now, that her condition has remained stable. I am getting used to it. She can never find her mouth and is covered with bruises, probably because she rams into the bars across her bed. I think of the silly expressions we use for children, like "You have a booboo?" or "Baby wants to go beddy-byes?"

Sunday 16

I hand her an almond bun; she can't eat it on her own, her lips suck wildly at thin air. Right now, I would like her to be dead and free of such degradation. Her body stiffens, she strains to stand up and a foul stench fills the atmosphere. She has just relieved herself like a newborn baby after being fed. Such horror and helplessness. Her right fist is clenched, her fingers digging deep into me—she also possesses the strength of a newborn baby.

Easter Sunday

It's her third Easter in this place. When I arrive, I always have trouble recognizing her because her face never looks the same. Today her mouth is twisted to the right. I have brought her a chocolate hen. The piece I break off is too big, she can't put the whole thing into her mouth; it slips out, she tries to catch it but clutches her chin instead. This scene, and all the other ones when she grabs at nothing, are the ones I find the most afflicting. After that, she kneads a lump of chocolate instead of bringing it to her lips, then makes a few unsuccessful attempts to eat it. By now she is smothered in chocolate. At this point, everything gets out of hand: horror has ceased to matter, it has even become necessary. Go on, spread it all over yourself, make a real mess of it. I can feel anger swelling up inside me, anger that comes straight from my childhood—an impulse to break everything, dirty everything and roll in the mud. Now this rage is directed against her. After I have fed her and wiped her mouth: "Do you still have all your teeth? Because my dentures are..." (the last word is muffled). I tell her not to worry, I'll have another set made; I tell her the first thing that comes into my head, like one does with children.

My mother's neighbor is in tears, sobbing in her wheelchair. I offer her a chocolate but she shakes her head, raising her ugly, puffed face. It breaks my heart. So does the following scene: as I bend forward to check the safety catch *of* my mother's wheelchair, she leans over and kisses my hair. How can I survive that kiss, such love, my mother, my mother.

A P R I L

Sunday 6

Her face exudes sweetness, there is no sign of the contracted jaws and haunted expression she's had in recent weeks. She had been dressed in long woolen socks that came up to her thighs. She raised her gown: her groin was covered in Mercurochrome, probably because, steeped in urine, the skin had become inflamed. Now she has "caught up" with the woman I saw here at Easter two years ago, who exposed her vagina shamelessly.

Monday 7

She is dead. I am overcome with grief. I haven't stopped crying since this morning. I don't grasp what's going on. That's it. Yes, time has stopped. One just can't imagine the pain. I long to see her again. This moment was something I had never imagined or foreseen. I preferred it when she was crazy.

I want to throw up, my head is aching. I had all that time to get closer to her and I didn't make the most of it. Not to have realized yesterday that I might be seeing her for the last time.

The bunch of forsythia I brought her yesterday was still on the table, in a jam jar. I had also brought her a bar of chocolate flavored with "forest fruits" and she had eaten the whole thing. I had shaved her face and sprinkled her body with eau de cologne. Now it's *all over*. She was "life itself." She would stretch out her hands to seize life.

She looks like a sad little doll. I gave the nurse the night-gown she wanted to be buried in—white cotton edged with lace. They won't let one do anything. I wanted to slip it on her myself.

I shall never hear the sound of her voice again.

I can't remember any of the words she said yesterday. Yes I can, she said to some visitors, "take a seat, make yourself comfortable," something like that.

Tuesday 8

A new day, one which will never dawn for her. She was life, nothing but life, and violence too. The weather is gray; I think of that new town that she never liked, where she died. Shall I ever recover from such pain?

Everything I do reminds me of her. Maybe I could consume my grief and wear it out by telling her story. I can't look at my notes, it's too painful. What I find most distressing is the gulf separating her two and a half years of decline, when she had grown so close to me, from her death. She had become a child again, one who would never grow up. Every time I went there, I wanted to feed her, clip her fingernails and comb her hair. Her clean, soft hair on Easter Sunday. One can't imagine that it will all be over one day.

Even today, it's not over yet.

Tomorrow I might throw a flower into her coffin or place a rosary between her hands. But no *written* text, no way.

I shudder at the thought of a book about her. Literature is so powerless.

I remembered Le Louvrais, that bleak district that she never took to, the Paris region where she lead an unhappy life. I feel like walking past the hairdresser's where I accompanied her in January 1984.

Now I must use the simple past, "she was" and so on. Last night, while I was trying to get to sleep, I thought, "It's the past perfect from now on." I keep recalling that last Sunday, the very last day.

Thursday 10

I feel panic-stricken, as if something were about to happen. I realize nothing can ever happen now.

"They're together now" (my father and mother), "she's better off where she is." Meaningless sentences that fail to move me; maybe one needs to say them anyway. At the butcher's this morning—the last time I went was "before it happened"—I was horrified by the meticulous care with which people chose their meat.

I saw myself sitting next to her last Sunday, reading about Roger Vadim's affair with Brigitte Bardot. At one point, she had reached out for the newspaper. The other lady wanted us to shut the door.

I went downstairs to the cellar. There was her suitcase, along with her purse, a white summer handbag and several scarves. I just stand there before the gaping suitcase and these scarce belongings. I don't know what I'm waiting for.

I don't want to open my mail, I am incapable of reading anything.

I know that I have experienced this condition only two or three times before in my life, after an unhappy love affair and after my abortion. Also, one Thursday afternoon, when I had "missed" her in Rouen. And when I had to leave her in Calais before taking the ferry for England in 1960.

I had accepted the fact that she was a little girl who would never grow up. For the first time, I understood a verse from a poem by Paul Éluard: "time is overflowing."

Everything people ask me to do—write articles, attend conferences—seems impossible and irrelevant.

The worst thing is to have written about her over the last two years, in her condition—a text for *Le Figaro* newspaper, a short story for the magazine *L'Autre Journal*, the diary of my hospital visits. Not to have thought that she might die.

I received a batch of essays to be corrected and graded. It doesn't annoy me like it usually does; I tell myself that I might just as well not look at them and that it doesn't really matter whether or not the corrections get done.

I believed she was going to die when I was five years old, when she made the pilgrimage to Lourdes.

I have searched for my mother's love in all corners of the world. This is not literature that I am writing. I can see the difference with my other books. Or rather, no I can't, for I am incapable of producing books that are not precisely that—an attempt to salvage part of our lives, to understand, but first to salvage. Over the phone, Annie M told me that it was impossible to express emotion directly; we need to resort to stratagems. I'm not so sure.

Love and hate. I wasn't able to tell her about my abortion. But that doesn't matter now.

I have to read the newspaper several times before grasping the meaning of an article. There is no book that I could face reading right now. Some would be unbearable because they chronicle what I have just experienced. Others are perfectly useless, mere fabrications.

I feel the urge to go back to the hairdresser's salon in the Cordeliers quarter, where I took her in January 1984.

I could also just sit here and wait, doing nothing, but somehow I can't.

In my present state, I could "sink even lower," I know that.

All the hardships I have endured were merely rehearsals to prepare me for this devastating pain.

Over the phone, I made an appointment to have the piano tuned. The woman says: "It's the 9th today. Oh no it's not, it's the 10th!" She laughs. There are plenty of people in the world who don't care whether it's the 9th or the 10th day of the month.

I dread reading through the "diary" of my visits to Pontoise Hospital.

I roam the house, telling myself that I should make the bed or cook a meal. Everything seems pointless. When I sit down at my desk, it's the only thing I can write about.

I did some gardening. It helped me to take my mind off things. I raked the earth and pulled out the weeds in the driveway. The weather is the same as when she was still alive—cold and misty.

Of course, I could wait before writing about my mother. I could wait until I have escaped from these days. But they are the truth, whatever that is.

When I used to write about her after getting back from the hospital, wasn't it a way of holding onto life?

Friday 11

I know that something is wrong because I need to read my students' papers several times before understanding them.

I'll have to tell her story in order to "distance myself

89

from it." I remembered there was a file with documents belonging to my mother in one of the drawers of my desk. I couldn't throw away all the papers, only a few of them. There was a slip confirming her application for a change of address when she moved to Cergy in September 1983.

My stomach suddenly starts acting up, like when I came across the slip of paper. I am incapable of doing anything although I know there is nothing to wait for.

The newspaper is the only thing I can read.

Maybe one day I'll read the notes I took after visiting her in the hospital and they will form a continuous sequence of events running from life to death. But for the moment, time has been severed: it stopped on Monday morning.

Saturday 12

In a letter of condolence from one of her friends in Annecy, I read: "That's life!" The expression means absolutely nothing to me.

Last week, while I was driving around, I decided that something nice would happen to me if I reached my destination before a certain time. Now I expect nothing.

I understand why a woman from our neighborhood who had lost her ten-month-old baby had spent the afternoon at the hairdresser's.

I am terrified to reread what I have written about her. And afraid to begin writing about the burial ceremony, or the last day when I saw her alive.

There are two days which I find it impossible to reconcile: a day like any other Sunday, when I went to see her, and the following day, Monday, the last day, the day of her death. Life and death remain separate, divided by some invisible barrier.

Right now I am experiencing this split notion of time. Hopefully, one day that feeling will end and everything will be reunited, like in a story. Before writing, I should probably wait until these two days have merged together in my own life.

I am going through this phase because for the past two and a half years (since the day I found her sleeping), I have desperately wanted her to live. I accepted her the way she was, in her state of decline.

Now the full meaning of that day is becoming clear to me. It was one evening in May, the sun was out. She was lying in bed, asleep. I thought back to my childhood and the Sunday afternoons when we would share the same bed. Then, in Sées in 1958, when I was shivering on my bed, obsessed with Claude G, and later with A, in 1984. One and only love.

As soon as I wake up, I immediately "know" that my

mother is dead. Every morning I emerge from her death. Yesterday I thought of the undertaker's assistant with his side parting, his head tilted to one side out of professional sympathy.

Sunday 13

The weather is still cold. Yesterday there was snow. The same thoughts when I wake up.

In the days following her death, all I could do was sob uncontrollably. Now the tears swell up unexpectedly, when I catch sight of some object or notice some small detail.

Today it's Sunday; for the first time I won't be going to the hospital between two and three o' clock this afternoon.

I had bought a bunch of forsythia for her in the village.

I feel more upset outdoors than indoors. As though I were searching for her outside. Outside, the world exists. Before, she too existed somewhere in the world.

September 1983. We are in her small apartment, sorting and throwing away papers before she moves into my place at Cergy. So it was already the beginning of the end.

I can't read through the pages I have just written.

Neither can I write a "real book" about her.

I tried to recollect every single detail about that last visit, as if something could be saved from oblivion.

Monday 14

This morning, I had the impression she was still alive. In the baker's, standing before the rows of cakes, I thought: "I don't need to buy those any more" and "I don't need to go to the hospital."

I recalled the popular melody "Les Roses Blanches,"[4] which always moved me to tears as a child. I start crying again, because of that song and its lyrics.

Wednesday 16

As soon as I settle at my desk, alone, I am overwhelmed by grief. I can speak only of her, to write about anything else would be impossible.

The first time I wrote "Mummy is dead" was agony. I could never write those words in a fictional work.

Sunday 20

I looked at some pictures of her, aged fifty. I feel certain she is still alive, bursting with health, with her reddish blond hair.

---

[4] A 1925 song with strong sentimental overtones: a little boy steals a bunch of white roses to take to his mother in the hospital but when he gets there he learns she has just died.

It's a black and white photograph but I see it in color, with the sun shining.

Between three and four o' clock, I felt like writing about the last time I saw her alive, exactly two weeks ago.

Monday 28

This morning, after seeing the words "cubic meter" on a water bill, I remembered that I used to call her Cubby when I was six or seven years old. Tears come to my eyes, thinking of time.